A BOY AND HIS DONKEY

Once there was a boy named Mark. Every morning Mark took his donkey to the forest to gather wood and every afternoon, before dark, Mark and his donkey returned home.

One day, the donkey decided he didn't want to go home and he sat down. "Come on," said Mark, "it's time to go!" But the donkey wouldn't budge. "It's time for dinner," said Mark, but still the donkey wouldn't budge.

As night fell, Mark felt very tired and very hungry. He wanted to go home, but the donkey wouldn't budge. So Mark sat down on a rock and began to cry. He cried and cried.

Just then a rabbit passed by. "Why are you crying?" asked the rabbit.

"I'm crying because I'm very tired and very hungry, and my donkey doesn't want to go home," said Mark.

"Don't cry," said the rabbit. "I'll talk to the donkey."

So the rabbit went up to the donkey and said, "Hey, it's getting dark, and it's time to go home. Let's race and see who can run home first."

But the donkey wouldn't budge.

Soon the rabbit grew tired of trying to get the donkey to move. He sat down next to Mark and started to cry, too.

There they were, the two of them, crying and crying, when a fox passed by.

"Why are you crying, rabbit?" asked the fox.

"I'm crying because the boy's crying, and the boy's crying because he's very tired and very hungry, and his donkey doesn't want to go home."

"Don't cry," said the fox. "I'll talk to the donkey."

So the fox went up to the donkey and said, "Hey, it's getting dark, and it's time to go home. Wild animals are coming out and they will eat you."

But the donkey wouldn't budge.

Soon the fox grew tired of trying to get the donkey to move. He sat down next to the rabbit and began to cry, too.

There they were, the three of them, crying and crying, when a wolf passed by.

"Why are you crying, fox?" asked the wolf.

"I'm crying because the rabbit's crying, because the boy's crying, because he's very tired and very hungry, and his donkey doesn't want to go home."

"Don't cry," said the wolf. "I'll talk to the donkey."

So the wolf went up to the donkey and said in a big, bad voice, "I am going to eat you. Get going!"

But the donkey wouldn't budge.

Soon the wolf grew tired of trying to get the donkey to move. He sat down next to the fox and began to cry, too.

There they were, the four of them, crying and crying, when a bee passed by.

"What a racket! What's going on?" she buzzed.

The wolf answered, "I'm crying because the fox's crying, because the rabbit's crying, because the boy's crying, because he's very tired and very hungry, and his donkey doesn't want to go home."

"What a lot of crying over nothing!" said the bee. "I'll go talk to the donkey."

At this, they all began to laugh. "You think you're going to convince the donkey? You – you tiny, little thing?" they all said.

"I'm a big, bad wolf and I can't scare him," said the wolf.

"I'm a crafty fox and I can't trick him," said the fox.

"I'm a speedy rabbit and I can't race him," said the rabbit.

"And I'm his master and I can't get him to do anything," said Mark.

So the bee went up to the donkey, buzzing, buzzing, zzzzz, zzzzz, zzzzz! The donkey saw the bee, but he wouldn't budge. The bee buzzed into his ear, zzzzz! And PING! She stung that donkey!

"Heeeeeee-haaaawwww!" brayed the donkey, and he jumped to his feet and ran home, with the bee zooming behind him all the way.